Library of Congress Cataloging in Publication Data

Edwards, Richard, 1949–Ten tall oak trees/by Richard Edwards:
illustrated by Caroline Crossland.—1st U.S. ed. p.–cm.
Summary: Over a period of time, a stand of ten oak trees is cut down
one by one, until there are none. [1. Oak—Fiction. 2. Trees—Fiction.
3. Counting. 4. Stories in rhyme.] I. Crossland, Caroline. ill.
II. Title. PZ8.3.E2854Te 1993 [E]—dc20 92-41771 CIP AC
ISBN 0-688-04620-7.—ISBN 0-688-04621-5 (lib. bdg.)
1 3 5 7 9 10 8 6 4 2
First U.S. edition

TEN TALL OAKTREES

Richard Edwards

pictures by Caroline Crossland

TAMBOURINE BOOKS • NEW YORK

Ten tall oaktrees
Standing in a line,
"Warships," cried King Henry,
Then there were nine.

Nine tall oaktrees
Growing strong and straight,
"Charcoal," breathed the furnace,
Then there were eight.

Eight tall oaktrees
Reaching toward heaven,
"Sizzle," spoke the lightning,
Then there were seven.

Seven tall oaktrees
Branches, leaves, and sticks,
"Firewood," smiled the merchant,
Then there were six.

Six tall oaktrees
Glad to be alive,
"Barrels," boomed the brewery,
Then there were five.

Five tall oaktrees
Suddenly a roar,
"Timber," screamed the west wind,
Then there were four.

Four tall oaktrees
Sighing like the sea,
"Floorboards," beamed the builder,
Then there were three.

Three tall oaktrees
Groaning as trees do,
"Unsafe," claimed the council,
Then there were two.

Two tall oaktrees
Spreading in the sun,
"Progress," snarled the highway,
Then there was one.

One tall oaktree
Wishing it could run,
"Nuisance," griped the farmer,
Then there were none.

No tall oaktrees
Search the fields in vain,
Only empty skylines,
And the cold gray rain.